igloobooks

Published in 2013
by Igloo Books Ltd
Cottage Farm
Sywell
NN6 0BJ
www.igloobooks.com

Copyright © 2012 Igloo Books Ltd.

FIR003 0713
6 8 10 9 7
ISBN 978-0-85780-435-8

Printed and manufactured in China

This igloo book belongs to:

....

It's Time To Play!

igloobooks

In the middle of the day, when the sun was very hot, Big Lion liked to lie down for a nice long nap.

Little Lion, who wanted to be just like Big Lion when he grew up, lay down, too.

Big Lion stretched right out and
fell fast asleep.

Little Lion stretched right out and
was wide awake.

Some beautiful butterflies fluttered past.
Little Lion watched them go, but …

… He couldn't help himself.
Off he went, chasing them as fast
as his little paws would carry him.

It was fun until…

… He fell over something big and furry!
"Wha… ? Woo… ! Owwww!" cried Big Lion.
"Little Lion, what are you doing?"

"I was doing my chasing practice," explained
Little Lion. "I want to run fast, like you do."

"Well, that's a good thing to do," sighed Big Lion,
"but this isn't a good time to do it.
Why don't you do something… slower?"

Big Lion lay down and was soon fast asleep.
Little Lion... slowly... looked around.

High in a nearby tree, a monkey
was hanging from a branch.

Little Lion climbed up the tree and tried
to move along the branch.

The branch wasn't very wide and it moved when Little Lion moved. Little Lion w o b b l e d.

"Ooooh… aaaah… ooooh!" he cried as he slipped…

…and fell onto something big and furry!

"Ooomf..! Foof..? Fwumf..!" gasped Big Lion.
"Little Lion! What are you doing?"

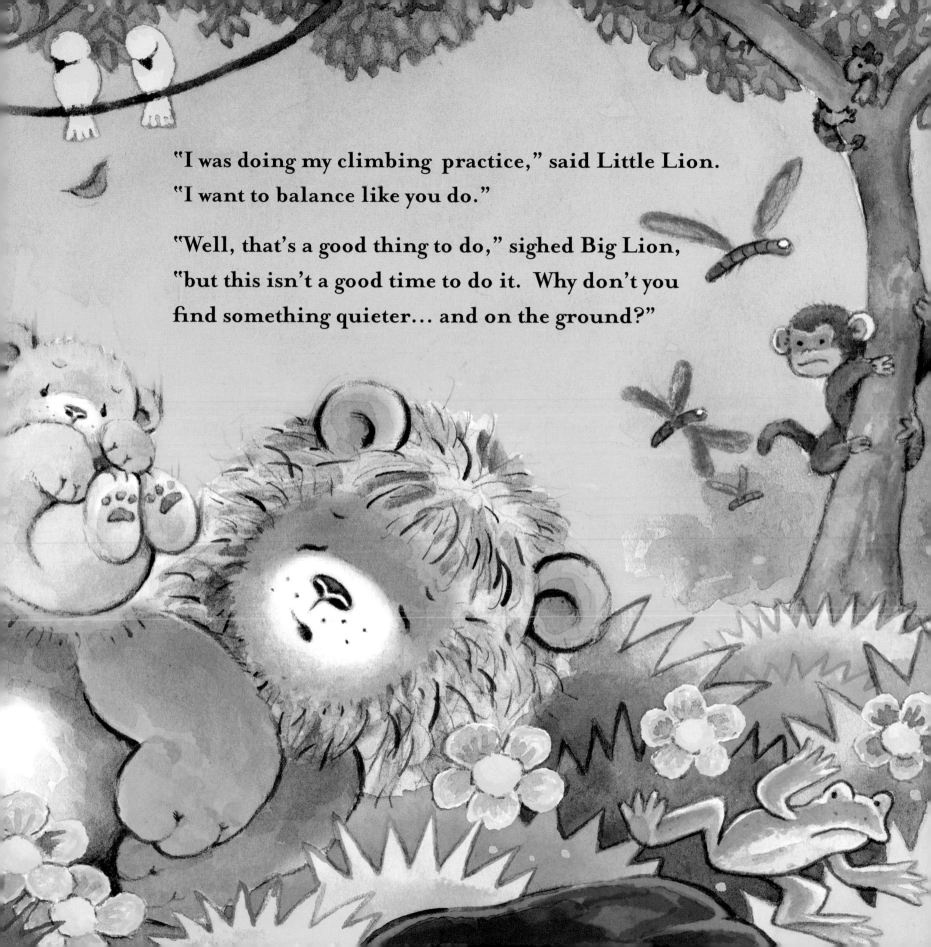

"I was doing my climbing practice," said Little Lion.
"I want to balance like you do."

"Well, that's a good thing to do," sighed Big Lion,
"but this isn't a good time to do it. Why don't you
find something quieter… and on the ground?"

So, Little Lion crept quietly through the grass, pretending he was brave and strong, like Big Lion.

Suddenly, he saw something wiggle right under his nose. Little Lion pounced!

"Ow …! Wah …? Ouch …!" cried Big Lion.
"Little Lion! What are you doing? That was my tail!"
"I was doing my creeping practice,"
said Little Lion. "I want to creep quietly,
like you do."

"Well," laughed Big Lion,
"I was doing my sleeping practice.
That's a good thing to do, but I don't think now
is a good time for me to do it.
Catch me if you can, Little Lion!"

All afternoon, Big Lion and Little Lion
played tag and hide-and-seek.
They weren't slow and they weren't quiet,
but they were sure of one thing.
It was a **very** good thing to do.